For Brock and Lev –
the two brightest of lights
~ N B

Let's celebrate together!
~ A S

IF YOU DON'T CELEBRATE CHANUKAH,
YOU MIGHT LIKE TO KNOW THAT . . .

This is the shamash. It's the "helper" candle and its job is to light the other candles, and share the light where it is needed.

This special candleholder is called a chanukiah – but many people call it a menorah! It is used for the celebration of Chanukah.

The menorah holds nine candles: one for each night of Chanukah, plus the shamash.

First American Edition 2022
Kane Miller, A Division of EDC Publishing

First published in Great Britain in 2022 by Little Tiger Press Ltd.,
an imprint of the Little Tiger Group

For information contact:
Kane Miller, A Division of EDC Publishing
5402 S 122nd E Ave
Tulsa, OK 74146
www.kanemiller.com
www.myubam.com

Library of Congress Control Number: 2021950005

ISBN 978-1-68464-441-4

Printed in China • LTP/2800/4449/0422
1 2 3 4 5 6 7 8 9 10

Eight Nights, Eight Lights

Natalie Barnes

Andrea Stegmaier

Kane Miller
A DIVISION OF EDC PUBLISHING

A dusting of frost forms across the busy city. The winter sun is starting to set, and shoppers are heading for home.

Chanukah, the festival of lights, is near.

"Hurry!" calls Max as he pulls on his grandpa's hand. "Tonight I get to light the first candle!"

When they reach the warmth of home, Max's grandma unwraps a special box.
Inside is a beautiful menorah.
"Small and silver. Old as time." She smiles.

The family gathers around and says prayers
as Max's mom helps him light the candle.

They sing traditional Hebrew songs.
Across the street, Lara's family
is singing them too.

The next day brings rain. Max and Lara splash through puddles as they race home from school.

"Today it's my turn to light the candles!" calls Lara, waving goodbye to Max.

From the kitchen wafts the smell
of delicious jelly donuts.

When there are too many . . .

. . . Lara and her dad share them
with their neighbors.

Later they return home, the two tall
candles in the window lighting their way.
The night grows colder and the first flakes
of snow start to fall . . .

. . . and by late afternoon the next day,
the streets wear a white blanket.

Ellie and Sam wait by the window.
Uncle Matthew, Aunt Lucy, and baby Lev
are coming to stay!
"His hands are so small!" whispers Ellie.

Food is shared, the chatter is loud.
Three candles dance in the kitchen window,
the room around them glowing with warmth.

On the fourth night of Chanukah,
four candles flicker and dance.

“Let’s play dreidel!” announces Uncle Matthew.
“I have a pocket full of chocolate coins,”
says Aunt Lucy, piling them on the rug.
Who will win? Sam spins the dreidel first.

“Hey, shin, nun . . .”

"Gimmel!" cheers Sam as he takes all
the chocolates in the pile.

He shares them with his family;
the gold foil shimmers bright . . .

. . . as bright as the sun that rises the next day. The sky over the city is as clear as glass, and the sidewalks are slick with ice.

"Whoa!" wobbles Mrs. Canning.

"Let's not fall over," says Mr. Canning, "before we deliver these donations and decorate our cookies."

"Ready for the party at the synagogue,"
they say together.

The Cannings' big, black cat pads to
his favorite spot in the living room.
Above his head, five candles blaze
as darkness falls once more.

A busy day has passed – from sunrise to sunset. Now, in their apartment, Yael, Meir, and Micah are opening their Chanukah gifts.

There is a book,

some stickers,

and a box of colored pencils!

Later, they help Dad make latkes.

The apartment is filled with the sound of oil popping in the pan.
The room glows with stories and laughter.

As six candles shine, old memories are shared . . .

. . . and by the next night, new ones are made.

David and Jillian have moved into their new home. They are surrounded by bags and boxes as night begins to fall.

"Found it!" Jillian shouts, pulling her mother's menorah out of a bag.

Tired, but happy, the couple light the seven candles together. Then they position the menorah on their windowsill and the bright light of Chanukah blesses their new house with love.

Seven nights of fun and friendship have passed.
Tonight is the eighth night.

The synagogue is busy with chatter.

But when Rabbi Rubin speaks, everyone listens.

He tells the story of Chanukah. How, long ago in Jerusalem, King Antiochus forced the Jewish people to give up their religion.

“Why?” Brock asks.

“He didn’t like the Jewish people,” Lauren whispers.

“So his guards destroyed the Temple and the jars of oil used to light the menorah.

But a brave family fought back . . .

And they won!

"They rebuilt the Temple and lit the menorah. There was enough oil for one night, but the lamp burned for eight nights. Just enough time to make more oil. It was a miracle! And it's why we light a candle for eight nights."

"Why was the king so mean?" asks Brock. Lauren says, "I think it was because he was scared. People can be scared when they see differences in others that they don't understand. But we are all different . . . that's what makes everyone special."

The eighth candle is lit.
Eight lights for eight nights.

Singing echoes throughout
the hall, and light pours out
of the synagogue onto
the dark street . . .

. . . as fireworks burst overhead.

Max looks out at his street. It is full of different houses, filled with many different people.

But their windows all burn bright with light.
And it looks beautiful.